A Christmas Carol

By **Charles Dickens**
Retold by **Pamela Kennedy**

Illustrated by **Carol Heyer**

Ideals Children's Books • Nashville, Tennessee

I dedicate this book with love to the memory of my parents—
William J. Heyer and Merlyn Heyer, who never failed to support
and encourage my imagination, creativity, and career.
—C.A.H

Thanks to David Atkinson, Suzan Davis Atkinson, and Ailsa Hutson.
Thanks also to the models and family who helped so much with this book:

Scrooge ....Charles Davis
Tiny Tim ....Zachary Guarino
Christmas Past...Richard Hallack
Money Boy...Steven Smith
Cratchit Boys...James Smith, Jeff Smith

Text copyright © 1995 by Hambleton-Hill Publishing, Inc.
Illustrations copyright © 1995 by Carol Heyer

Published by Ideals Children's Books
An imprint of Hambleton-Hill Publishing, Inc.
Nashville, Tennessee 37218

Printed and bound in Mexico

Library of Congress Cataloging-in-Publication Data
Kennedy, Pamela.
      A Christmas carol / retold by Pamela Kennedy from the original by Charles
Dickens ; illustrated by Carol Heyer.
            p.   cm.
      Summary: A simplified retelling of how the miserly Scrooge learns the true meaning
of Christmas when three ghostly visitors review his past and foretell his future.
      ISBN 1-57102-047-0
      [1. Christmas—Fiction. 2. Ghosts—Fiction. 3. England—Fiction] I. Heyer, Carol,
1950– ill. II. Dickens, Charles, 1812–1870. Christmas carol. III. Title.
PZ7.K3849Ch   1995
[Fic]—dc20   95-9990
                                                                           CIP
                                                                            AC

The illustrations in this book were rendered in acrylics using live models.
The text type was set in Goudy.
The display type was set in Goudy Lombardic Text.
Color separations were made by Color 4, Inc.
Printed and bound by R.R. Donnelley & Sons

First Edition
10 9 8 7 6 5 4 3 2 1

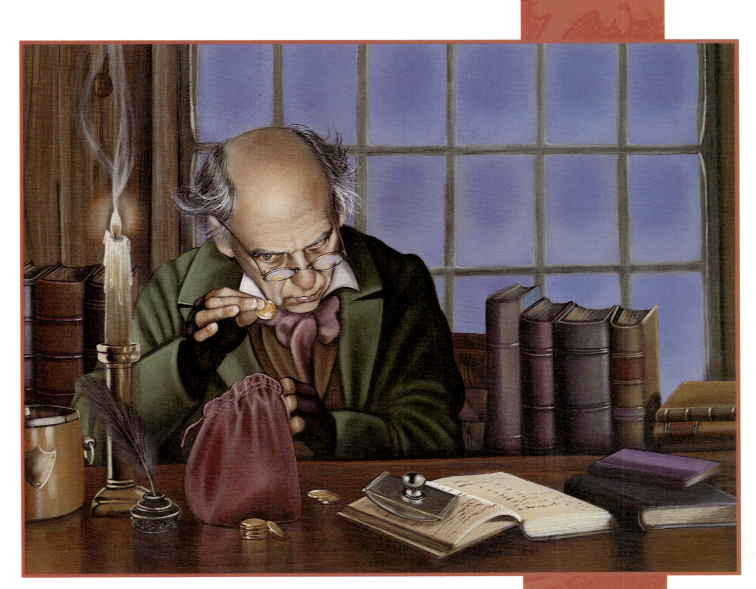

Marley was dead, as dead as a doornail. And even though he had been dead for seven years, Scrooge had never painted out Jacob Marley's name above the countinghouse door.

Oh! I tell you, he was a tight-fisted man, that Scrooge! A squeezing, grasping, scraping, clutching, selfish old sinner! He was as hard as stone. The cold inside him gave him a frosty look on even the warmest days. Even his words were sharp and cold as ice and matched very well the frosty white hair on his head.

Now once upon a time on Christmas Eve, Scrooge sat counting out his money in his countinghouse. It was a terribly cold and very foggy night.

The door of Scrooge's office was open so he could keep an eye upon his clerk, Bob Cratchit, who was busy copying letters. Poor Bob was wrapped in a long wool muffler, for Scrooge was too stingy to allow him a fire.

With a sudden gust of winter wind, the door of the chilly countinghouse flew open. In marched Scrooge's nephew. "Merry Christmas, Uncle! God save you!"

"Bah!" growled Scrooge. "Humbug!"

"Christmas a humbug, Uncle? Surely you don't mean it," the nephew replied. "Why don't you come have Christmas dinner with us tomorrow. Enjoy yourself for once."

"No!" shouted Scrooge. "I do not wish to enjoy myself. Now go your way and leave me alone!"

"Well, Merry Christmas anyway, Uncle. And a Happy New Year too," the nephew sang out gaily as he headed out the door.

"Bah humbug!" Scrooge shouted crossly as he watched his nephew disappear and then returned to his counting.

The door had hardly closed when it was pushed open again and two smiling, well-dressed gentlemen entered. They bowed politely as they took off their hats.

"Good day, kind sir," the taller one said cheerfully. "A few of us are trying to raise some money to buy the poor some food and drink and ways to keep warm. We chose this time because Christmas is a time for giving. What shall I put you down for?"

"Nothing!" Scrooge replied.

"You wish to give in secret?"

"I wish to be left alone!" said Scrooge. "If these folks you talk about are poor, I'm sure it is because they are lazy. If they do not care to work, then let them starve or go to the poorhouse. Either way, it is no concern of mine. Good afternoon."

Faced with these angry words, the two men backed away. They shook their heads, put on their hats, and left the gloomy countinghouse.

Scrooge turned to look at his bundled up clerk who sat on his high stool, grinning.

"And I suppose you'll want all day tomorrow off," the old man snapped.

"If it isn't too much trouble, sir," the clerk replied.

"Well, it is too much trouble!" Scrooge said. "I pay you to work." He buttoned his overcoat to his chin. "I suppose you may have it off," he added grudgingly. Then he shook his finger at the man. "But you'd better be here early the next day."

The clerk promised he would be in early and Scrooge stomped out, slammed the door, and headed home.

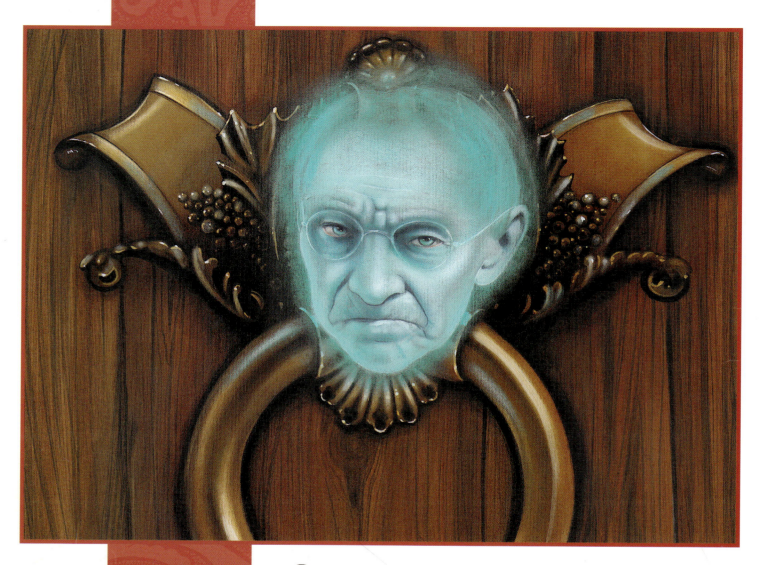

𝔑ow the door to Scrooge's house had a very large brass knocker. As Scrooge began to turn the key in the old door lock, he happened to look at the knocker. At first he blinked. The knocker looked strange. There was an eerie light. Then, from the center of the knocker glowed a ghostly face with ghostly spectacles on its ghostly forehead. It looked as Marley used to look!

Scrooge's spine tingled and his hair stood up. Then, as he stared at the ghostly face, it became a knocker again. Trembling, he shook his head. He dashed in the house, ran up the stairs, and went straight to his room. Once there, he locked the door twice, then put on his dressing gown, slippers, and nightcap.

Scrooge served himself a bowl of thin gruel and huddled before his small fire. It gave so little heat that he had to crouch down to feel its warmth. But another handful of fuel would cost money, and he'd rather suffer than spend a cent. As he sat there alone, his mind returned to the face in the knocker. "Humbug," he said to himself.

No sooner had he said this than strange things began to happen—things I am almost afraid to tell. An old bell hanging in the corner began to ring all by itself. He heard footsteps coming up the stairs and chains clanking across the floors, coming closer, closer, closer.

Then suddenly, right through the twice-locked door came a strange ghost. It stood there dressed in Marley's coat and wearing Marley's boots, but wrapped all around with chains made of keys and locks, cashboxes and bankbooks.

Scrooge sat frozen. He felt the chill of the ghost's eyes. "Who are you?" he whispered. "What do you want with me?"

"Much," said Marley's voice, and Scrooge trembled.

"Why do you trouble me?" he asked.

"I have wandered over the earth for seven years," said the ghost, "weighed down by these awful chains. When I lived I cared only about money and bankbooks. I never said a kind word to a needy soul. I never gave a poor beggar a cent. I lived a wasted and selfish life and now I must wander like this forever. I am here to warn you that you still have a chance to escape my fate, Ebenezer."

Scrooge shivered.

"You will be haunted," the ghost went on, "by three spirits. The first will arrive tomorrow when the clock strikes one. You will see me no more, but for your own sake, remember what I have said."

The ghost of Jacob Marley moved slowly toward the window, and the window opened by itself. As if pulled by a dreadful force, Scrooge followed the ghost to the window. As Marley slipped out into the foggy night, the air was suddenly filled with ghostly creatures. They cried and wailed, moaned and wept. Terror seized Scrooge and he slammed the window shut, then stood there trembling. He looked at the still twice-locked door. He tried to say "humbug" but the word would not come out. Then he turned from the fire, went straight to bed, and fell asleep in an instant.

When Scrooge awoke, he saw nothing at first. In the stillness of the night, he heard a clock chime ONE. Suddenly, beside his bed stood a strange figure—like a child in size, but like an old man in appearance. It had long white hair but fair smooth skin without a single wrinkle. From its head a beam of light glowed brightly. It wore a white tunic with a shining belt and carried a branch of holly in its hand.

Scrooge held his blankets up to his chin and asked, "Are you the Spirit whose coming was foretold to me?"

"Yes," it said. "I am the Ghost of Christmas Past. Rise, and walk with me!"

In an instant the Spirit carried Scrooge to the office where he had worked as a young man.

"Why, it's Old Fezziwig!" exclaimed Scrooge.

As he watched, his old boss slapped a much younger Scrooge on the back and said, "No more work tonight, it's Christmas Eve. Come, young Ebenezer, let's clear the floor and set up for a party!"

The men set to work. The floor was swept, the lamps were trimmed, and wood was heaped on the fire. Laughing people came in through the door. The orchestra began to play and the tables were spread with good things to eat. Couples danced and sang and laughed the night away.

Watching this delightful scene, Scrooge's mind wandered to another Christmas past. A fair young girl in a pale silk dress sat beside him. Her eyes were filled with tears.

"I cannot marry you, Ebenezer," she said softly, "for you love another more than I."

"There is no one else," Scrooge argued.

"Not someone, but something," she said. "You love your money more than you love me."

"Money is important," Scrooge said. He tried to hold her hand, but she stood to go.

She looked at him sadly, with pity in her eyes. "I hope you will be happy in the life you have chosen, Ebenezer." A single tear ran down her cheek, and then she turned and left.

Watching this scene from a long ago Christmas, Scrooge felt his heart ache. "Spirit!" he cried. "Show me no more. Take me home. Why do you torture me?"

"Come then," the Spirit answered. "I don't have much time. We must return."

Instantly Scrooge was back in his own room. The last thing he saw was the departing Spirit. Then he fell on his bed in a heavy sleep.

In the middle of a loud snore, Scrooge sat up in bed. He hardly had time to think before the clock struck one again. Looking around, he saw a light in the next room. Slowly he rose and walked to the door. As he placed his hand on the knob, he heard his name called. The door swung open, and he walked through.

It was his own room—but it looked very different. The walls and ceiling were hung with deep green boughs of holly. The crisp leaves and bright berries glistened cheerfully. A blazing fire filled the room with brightness. Heaped on the floor was a steaming and fragrant feast.

Seated on this heap of delicacies was an enormous, laughing giant. "Come in!" he boomed. "I am the Ghost of Christmas Present." He was dressed in a flowing green robe and wore a crown of holly and icicles. His brown curls were long and free. His eyes sparkled. His voice was filled with good cheer. He reached out his hand toward a shivering and bewildered Scrooge and commanded, "Touch my robe."

Scrooge touched the robe and was whisked with the Spirit through the walls of his house and along the snowy streets until they arrived at the home of poor Bob Cratchit.

It was a simple house, yet Scrooge noticed that the very air was filled with life. The fire crackled, the pots bubbled, the candlelight danced, and five young Cratchits and their mother bustled around excitedly.

"Where's your father?" asked Mrs. Cratchit. "And where is your brother, Tiny Tim?"

The children raced to the frosty window to see into the dark night. Before long the younger ones cried, "Here he is! Here's Father!"

Through the opened door came Bob, his long muffler hanging down before him, and Tiny Tim on his shoulder. Poor Tiny Tim was pale and thin. He carried a little crutch and his legs were supported by an iron brace.

"Come now," urged Mrs. Cratchit. When all were seated, she served the Christmas feast. There were warm baked apples and boiled potatoes and heaps of fragrant dressing. There was a fine plump goose with golden gravy, and after all had eaten well—a pudding topped with holly!

At the end of the meal, Bob Cratchit raised his cup and said, "A Merry Christmas to us all, my dears. God bless us!"

"God bless us every one!" cried Tiny Tim.

He sat very close to his father's side, on his little stool. Bob held his small hand in his, for he loved the child, and wished to keep him by his side. He was afraid that Tiny Tim might not live to see another Christmas.

"Spirit," said Scrooge, "tell me if Tiny Tim will live."

"I see an empty seat," replied the Ghost, "and a crutch without an owner. If these shadows remain unchanged by the future, the child will die."

"No, no," said Scrooge, "Oh, no, kind Spirit! Say he will be spared!"

"If all remains unchanged, no one will find him here," the Spirit answered sadly. "Come along."

Everywhere they went that night, the Spirit left his blessing and tried to teach Scrooge how to do the same. But time passed quickly, and when the clock struck one again, the joyful Spirit disappeared.

Frightened, Scrooge peered into the darkness all around him. He called out, but no one answered. He was all alone. Then, in the distance, he saw a dark and frightening shape. It was dressed in a hooded cape and moved like a shadowy mist toward him. The Spirit's black robe hid its form completely, except for one bony, outstretched hand. The air was filled with gloom, and Scrooge found it hard to breathe. A gust of wind stirred the Ghost's robe and Scrooge gasped at what he saw. From beneath the shadowy hood, two ghostly eyes pierced him with an icy glare.

"Are you the Ghost of Christmas Yet to Come?" asked Scrooge in a terrified whisper.

The Spirit said nothing, but nodded slightly and pointed straight ahead. It began to move and Scrooge followed in its shadow, carried along by the dark robe.

They came to the home of Bob Cratchit. Scrooge saw the family gathered around a little fire—sitting quietly, very quietly. Tiny Tim's empty chair was in the corner.

"Will Father be home soon?" one of the children asked.

"It's past the time he usually comes," said another. "He used to walk home quickly, even with Tiny Tim upon his shoulder."

"He walks so slowly these days," said their mother sadly.

Then the door swung open and in came Bob Cratchit, his old muffler wrapped around his neck. The children ran to him, and Scrooge watched as the family embraced.

"Oh, Father, whatever shall we do without our Tiny Tim?" cried one of the girls.

Bob wiped a tear from his eye. "We shall not forget him. And when we do remember him, we shall recall how patient and kind he was, although he was a little, little child."

The family kissed and held each other.

Then the Spirit carried Scrooge away. They passed from one place to another, but Scrooge never saw himself. All at once the Spirit stopped beside an iron gate. The gate opened on a churchyard that was old and choked with weeds. The Spirit glided in among the graves and stopped, pointing with its bony hand at one neglected stone.

Scrooge clutched his chest. His throat went dry. His heart began to pound. Slowly dread, like icy fingers, crept along his spine. "Who is it? Who lies there?" he gasped.

But the Ghost just stood, pointing, and never said a word.

Slowly, slowly, Scrooge crept toward the dark and dreary grave. His legs were weak. His teeth were clenched. His heart thumped in his ears. Then a beam of moonlight struck the stone. In deeply carved granite he read his name—EBENEZER SCROOGE.

He shrieked and fell upon the Ghost's dark robe. "Oh no, oh no! Oh, hear me Spirit, hear me! Tell me I may have a hope of changing what you've shown me. I am not the man I was. Have pity, Spirit!" Scrooge rose to his knees at the Spirit's feet. "I will honor Christmas in my heart and try to keep it all the year! I will live in the Past, the Present, and the Future. I will listen to the lessons they all teach. Help me change the future!"

In his agony, he caught the Spirit's hand; but as he did, the hand shrank, collapsed, and changed into a bedpost.

Yes, and the bedpost was his own. The bed was his own, the room was his own. Best and happiest of all, the time before him was his own.

"I *will* live in the Past, Present, and Future," Scrooge repeated as he scrambled joyfully out of bed. "Oh, thank you, Jacob Marley! Thank you, most sincerely."

Scrooge was in such a hurry to put on his clothes that he got them all inside out and upside down! He kept jumping about and shouting, "I'm as light as feather, as happy as an angel, as merry as a schoolboy! I don't even know what day it is!"

Running to the window, he threw it open and put out his head. No fog, no mist, just clear bright air—golden with sunlight and merry with bells.

"What's today?" called Scrooge to a boy passing by.

"Today?" replied the boy. "Why it's Christmas Day!"

"It's Christmas!" said Scrooge to himself. "I haven't missed it. The spirits have done it all in one night!"

"You, boy," called Scrooge again, "you know the prize turkey hanging down at the market?"

"Yes, sir," answered the boy.

"What a bright boy you are," exclaimed Scrooge, "what a delightful, intelligent boy! Here!" Scrooge gave the boy a handful of money. "Now run and buy that turkey and take it to the Bob Cratchit house. Here's some extra for you. Now run along!"

The surprised boy took the money and was off in a rush.

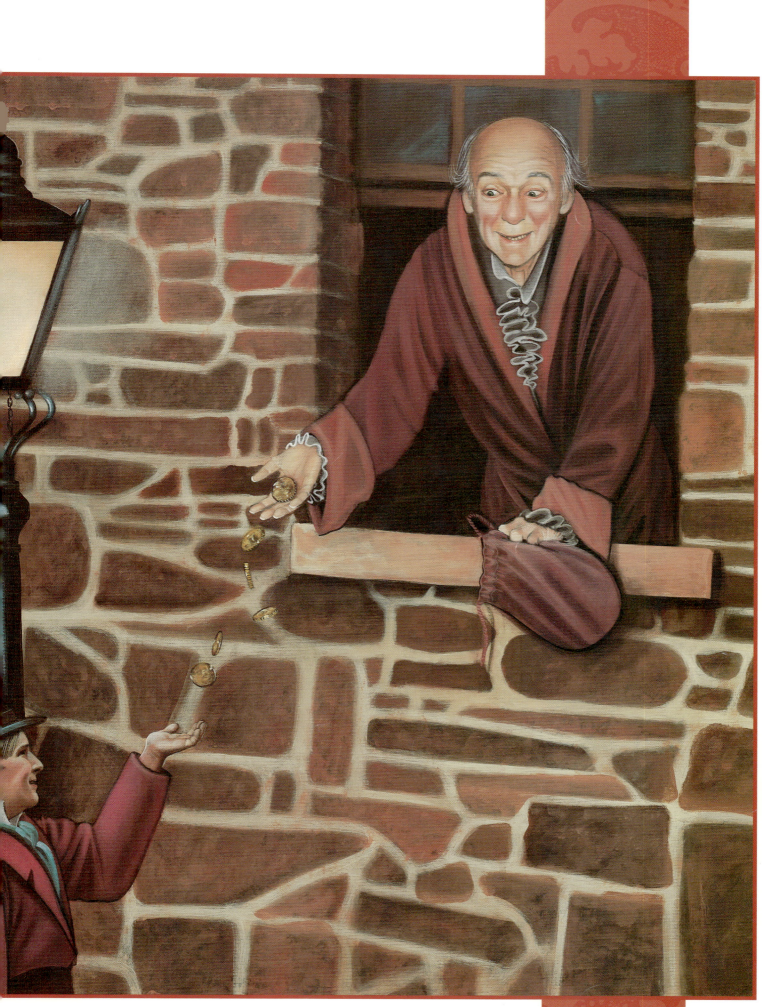

Scrooge was so pleased with himself and his idea that he laughed out loud. Grabbing his coat and his hat, he ran outside and down the street calling "Merry Christmas" to all he passed.

Turning a corner, he almost crashed headlong into the two gentlemen who had visited his office the day before. "Oh, what luck!" cried Scrooge as he took the taller one by both hands.

"I hope your fund for the poor has met with great success, but in case it hasn't, please stop by my office tomorrow and I'll write you a check for whatever amount you'd like."

The gentlemen stuttered with surprise.

Scrooge waved his hand, "No need to say thanks. It's Christmas, you know. Time to be thinking of the less fortunate!"

With that he dashed off, singing a bit of a Christmas carol as he went.

The next morning Scrooge was at his countinghouse early, for he hoped to catch Bob Cratchit coming in late. And sure enough, he did. Poor Bob came rushing in at twenty minutes past nine, frightened and cold.

"Late, humph!" growled Scrooge. "Come in here, Cratchit!" He tried to sound as mean and cross as usual.

"Oh, sir, please forgive me. It won't happen again. I promise, sir," poor Bob begged.

Scrooge glared at the shivering clerk, "I'm not going to stand for this kind of thing any longer!" He paused for a moment, then went on with a grin. "And therefore, I'm about to raise your pay! Merry Christmas, Bob. I'll not only pay you more, but I'll help your family. Now go build a big fire so you don't freeze to death."

And Ebenezer Scrooge was better than his word. He did it all and even more; and to Tiny Tim, who did not die, he was a second father. He became as good a friend, as good a boss, and as good a man as anyone ever knew.

Some people laughed to see the change in Scrooge, but he didn't care. His heart was filled with joy and that was enough for him. From that day on, it was always said that Ebenezer Scrooge knew how to keep Christmas well.

And may that be said of each of us. And so, as Tiny Tim observed: *God bless us every one!*